Henry

Based on
The Railway Series
by the
Rev. W. Awdry

Illustrations by
Robin Davi
Jerry Sr

D1331875

EGMON

EGMONT
We bring stories to life

First published in Great Britain in 2016
by Egmont UK Limited
The Yellow Building, 1 Nicholas Road, London W11 4AN

Thomas the Tank Engine & Friends™

CREATED BY BRITT ALLCROFT
Based on the Railway Series by the Reverend W Awdry
© 2016 Gullane (Thomas) LLC. Thomas the Tank Engine & Friends and
Thomas & Friends are trademarks of Gullane (Thomas) Limited.
Thomas the Tank Engine & Friends and Design is Reg. U.S. Pat. & Tm. Off.
© 2016 HIT Entertainment Limited.

HiT entertainment

ISBN 978 1 4052 7977 2
62418/1
Printed in Italy

Stay safe online. Egmont is not responsible for content hosted by third parties.

Written by Emily Stead. Designed by Claire Yeo.
Series designed by Martin Aggett.

FSC
MIX
Paper
FSC® C018306

Egmont is passionate about helping to preserve the world's remaining ancient forests.
We only use paper from legal and sustainable forest sources.

This book is made from paper certified by the Forest Stewardship Council® (FSC®),
an organisation dedicated to promoting responsible management of forest resources.
For more information on the FSC, please visit www.fsc.org. To learn more about Egmont's
sustainable paper policy, please visit www.egmont.co.uk/ethical

*This story is about my friend
Henry, the Number 3 green engine.
Henry may look strong, but he was
often ill and couldn't work.
Then he tried some special
coal and felt as
good as new . . .*

Henry was a big engine but sometimes he didn't feel strong enough to pull trains.

One morning, Henry was feeling very sorry for himself.

"My **axles ache** and my **tank** is **tingling**," he cried.

"Rubbish, Henry," huffed James. "You don't work hard enough."

The Fat Controller was worried.

"You are **always** at the Steamworks, Henry," The Fat Controller explained. "But new parts and a new coat of paint have done you no good. If we can't make you better we will have to find another engine instead."

Henry felt very sad.

Henry tried his best to pull the train that day, but it was no good. He didn't have enough steam.

"Now I shall be sent away," Henry worried.

He steamed **slowly** into a siding and Edward took his coaches.

The next day The Fat Controller was waiting for Henry. He wasn't wearing his top hat and coat – he had put on his overalls. He climbed onto Henry's footplate.

Henry's fire was lit, but his Fireman wasn't happy.

"Henry is a bad steamer," he told The Fat Controller. "His fire never gets **hot** enough."

The Fat Controller asked the Fireman what he thought was wrong with Henry.

"It's the coal, Sir," the Fireman said. "It's fine for engines with big fireboxes, but Henry's is small and can't make enough heat. He needs special Welsh coal."

"It's expensive," said The Fat Controller. "But we **must** help Henry."

Henry and his crew were very excited when the new coal arrived.

"Now we'll show them, Henry!" they said.

They oiled Henry's joints and polished him from **funnel** to **footplate**.

Henry whistled happily. **"PEEP! PEEP!"**

Henry's Fireman built a roaring fire and soon Henry's **boiler** was **bubbling**.

"PEEP! PEEP! PEEP!" whistled Henry. "I feel fantastic!" he told The Fat Controller.

He let off some steam with a great **"WHEEEESH!"**

Henry was impatient. His wheels were **ready to roll!**

"Don't go too quickly," The Fat Controller warned Henry's Driver.

"Yes, Sir," the Driver replied.

As Henry **steamed** all over Sodor, he had never felt better.

He wanted to go even **faster** but his Driver had promised not to.

"Steady, Henry," said his Driver. "There's plenty of time."

But they still arrived early at the station. Thomas puffed in soon after Henry.

"What kept you, lazybones?" **whooshed** Henry.

Before Thomas could answer, Henry sped off again. "I can't wait for slow tank engines like you!" Henry called cheekily.

Henry was very happy. With his special coal,
he could work as hard as any engine.

Then one day Henry was given a new shape and
a bigger firebox.

Now Henry is so **splendid** and **strong** that he
sometimes pulls the Express . . . and he doesn't
need special coal any more.

"Hooray for Henry!" his passengers all cheer.

More about Henry

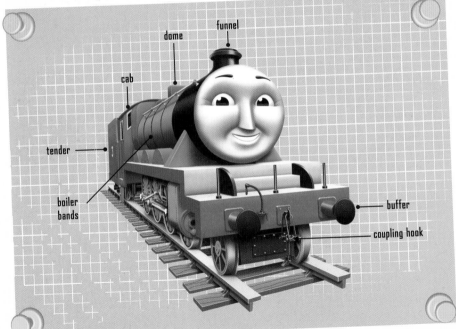

cab

dome

funnel

tender

boiler
bands

buffer

coupling hook

Henry's challenge to you

Look back through the pages of this book
and see if you can spot:

oil can

bird

sheep

passenger

spade

THE **THOMAS** *ENGINE ADVENTURES*

From Thomas to Harold the Helicopter, there is an Engine Adventure to thrill every Thomas fan.

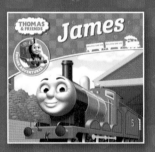

James

Spencer

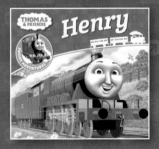

Henry

Thomas

Percy

Harold

E2595